Dandelion's
burrow

stream

Washing line

reading
garden

pond

greenhouse

Emma Thomson's
DANDELION

Dandelion's Day
by Emma Thomson

British Library Cataloguing in Publication Data
A catalogue record of this book is available from
the British Library.
ISBN 0 340 88404 5 (HB)

First edition published 2005
10 9 8 7 6 5 4 3 2 1

Published by Hodder Children's Books
a division of Hodder Headline Limited
338 Euston Road London NW1 3BH

Printed in China

Emma Thomson's
DANDELION

Dandelion's Day

*h*

Hodder
Children's
Books

A division of Hodder Headline Limited

In a quiet corner of Emma's garden,
by a trickling stream, lives a
little rabbit called Dandelion.
His burrow is at the base
of an old chestnut tree.

Dandelion is not much bigger
than a plant pot, even when
he stands on his tiptoes!
But he is the perfect size to
squeeze in and out of his burrow.

Every morning Dandelion
washes his long velvety ears with his
paws. Then he bounces softly
to the vegetable patch for
his breakfast.

With his tummy full to pop,
Dandelion hops happily through
the field to visit his friends.
He shares Emma's garden with
butterflies, snails, ladybirds and bees.

There's a special bee called Cecily
who is Dandelion's best friend.
She follows him everywhere, humming
tunes in his long floppy ears!

Dandelion's favourite game is hide-and-seek in the daisies. But wherever he hides, Cecily always gives him away.

Playing games soon makes
Dandelion feel a little sleepy.
And he hops into his favourite
plant pot to softly snooze
in the afternoon sun.

When he awakes Dandelion is
so full of energy that Cecily has
trouble keeping up with him.
He bounces everywhere, until he
finally ends up in a big green boot!

But nothing is as much fun
as showing off his new
trick to Cecily.

Daisy the duck waddles over to see what all the noise is about. "Nothing much," says Dandelion, looking up at her with an innocent smile.

As the sun begins to sink
Dandelion's day is almost at an end.
He waves goodbye to all his friends
and hops back home to his
cosy burrow.

When the moon comes up
Emma's garden is silent and still.
Dandelion is sound asleep,
dreaming of another day…

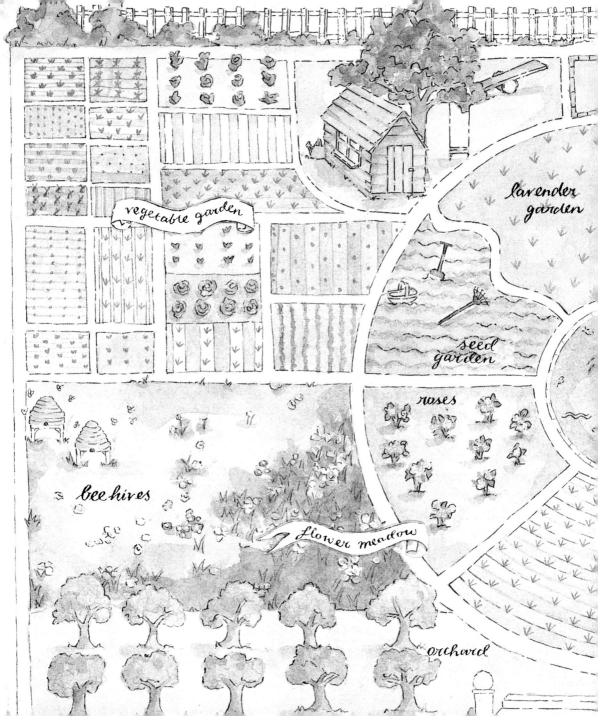

vegetable garden

lavender garden

seed garden

roses

bee hives

flower meadow

orchard